Jordi's Star

ALMA FLOR ADA

ILLUSTRATED BY SUSAN GABER

G. P. PUTNAM'S SONS / NEW YORK

Per a tu, Quica,
fins a la lluny del mar.
A. F. A.

For Paul Viviano
S. G.

Although *Jordi's Star* reads as a folktale, it is an original story.
The author's love for folktales has lent the story its flavor of a
traditional tale.

Jordi is a popular name in Catalonia. Saint Jordi is the patron
saint of Catalonia. To celebrate Saint Jordi's feast day, April 23,
friends greet each other with the traditional gift of a rose and
a book.

The artwork was done with acrylics on coquille board.

Text copyright © 1996 by Alma Flor Ada
Illustrations copyright © 1996 Susan Gaber
All rights reserved. This book, or parts thereof, may not be reproduced in any form
without permission in writing from the publisher. G .P. Putnam's Sons, a division of
The Putnam & Grosset Group, 200 Madison Avenue, New York, NY 10016.
G. P. Putnam's Sons, Reg. U.S. Pat. & Tm. Off. Published simultaneously in Canada.
Printed in Hong Kong by South China Printing Co. (1988) Ltd.
Book designed by Gunta Alexander. Text set in Aurelia.

Library of Congress Cataloging-in-Publication Data
Ada, Alma Flor. Jordi's star / by Alma Flor Ada; illustrated by Susan Gaber.
    p.   cm.   Summary: A lonely shepherd sees a star floating on the surface of a
small pool and, convinced that the star is really in the water, tries to make the
mountainside beautiful for its new resident.   [1. Shepherds—Fiction.
2. Stars—Fiction.]   I. Gaber, Susan, ill. II. Title.   PZ7.S1857Sh   1996
[Fic]—dc20   95—11048   CIP   AC

ISBN 0-399-22832-2   10 9 8 7 6 5 4 3 2 1   First Impression

Every day, Jordi chased his small herd of goats over the bare rocky hills, where a forest once stood. Long before, woodcutters had cut down all of the trees, and the rains had washed away all but a few stubborn weeds.

When Jordi needed water, he had to climb all the way down to the river to fetch it. He had tried digging a hole in the ground near his hut, thinking he might open a well. But no matter how deep he dug, the earth remained dry.

One windy afternoon, dark clouds settled over the mountain. Lightning bolts struck the rocky slopes as Jordi struggled to gather his small herd of goats and seek shelter in a cave.

Inside the shepherd mumbled to himself: "So much water all in one day!" He was glad he had remembered to leave a bucket outside his hut to catch the rain. "At least tomorrow I won't have to walk down to the river for water."

When the storm was over, Jordi started for home. The goats had not had enough to eat and bleated their complaints the whole way home, and the muddy ground made the journey all the more difficult.

At last, Jordi finished herding the goats into their pen and made his way to his hut past the hole he had been digging with such high hopes.

In the aftermath of the storm, a pool of water had formed. The stars shone brightly in the clear night sky. And there, in the still waters of the pool, was a bright and shining light.

Maybe it was because Jordi was so tired. Or maybe it was because he was alone so much, seeing other people only twice a month when he made his way to town in order to sell cheese. Or maybe it was because Jordi had lived all of his life on these rocky slopes. In any case, when Jordi saw the star, he thought that it had truly fallen into the water, and that it was really there, floating on the surface of his small pool.

Jordi felt an immense joy. Overcome with happiness, he knelt beside the water. Completely forgetting how tired he was, he spent a long time gazing at the star.

The next morning, the first thing Jordi did was dash outside to visit the pool. The water was clear and still, reflecting the blue sky above, but the star was nowhere to be found.

"She went to sleep, poor dear," thought Jordi. "Surely she must have gone down to the bottom of the pool, and that's why I don't see her. I wonder if she likes living here."

And so, before he set out with the goats for the day, Jordi rolled a large rock to the edge of the pond. Later, while the goats grazed, he found a bit of moss between some rocks. He gathered the moss, thinking that maybe the star would like the softness.

Jordi thought about the star the whole way home. After he had penned the goats, he moved another rock next to the first, and placed the moss between the two.

At last darkness fell, and Jordi ran to see if the star had appeared on the surface of the pool once more.

"I knew you were there all along," Jordi whispered softly. "Did you sleep well?" He gazed tenderly at the star for a long, long time. And that night, Jordi smiled in his sleep.

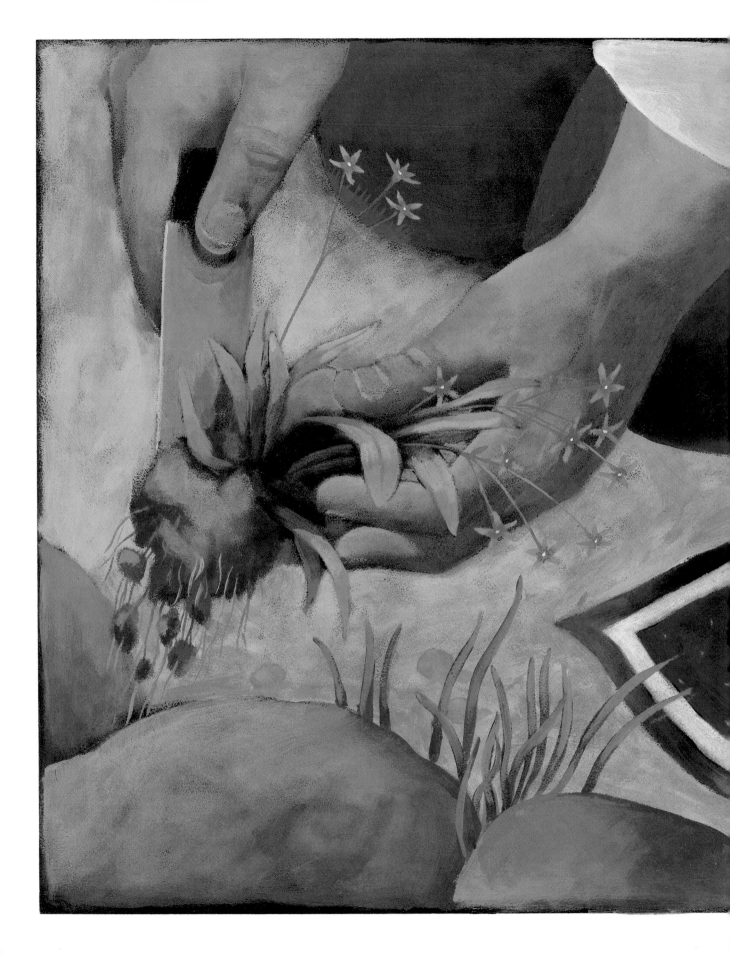

The next day, Jordi placed another rock next to the water before he left with the goats. Later, while his goats wandered about, he wondered if he might find something even more special for his star.

First he found a small quartz stone, white and brilliant. Then he found some tiny blue flowers that he had never noticed before, growing between some rocks. He used his knife to carefully dig out a clump of earth from underneath the flowers, so as to not damage their roots. Then he wrapped the tiny plants in his kerchief.

When he returned home that evening, Jordi planted the flowers next to the pool and dropped the quartz pebble into the water. The white quartz sparkled from the bottom of the pool, and when Jordi saw how bright his star shone that night, he thought that she must surely be thanking him for having brought her such a lovely present.

The next day, Jordi filled his pockets with quartz pebbles. In the evening, he let them drop one by one to the bottom of the pool. Day by day, Jordi placed more rocks around the edge of the pool, forming a wall. Between each rock he placed some moss in order to bind the rocks together. When the next storm came the water level rose, and the little pool began to turn into a small pond whose bottom shone with a thousand quartz pebbles.

When Jordi went to town later that month to sell some of his goat's milk cheese, he returned with all kinds of things to plant. One of his clients was pruning some apple trees, and Jordi asked him for some cuttings. Another client gave him some rose seedlings, while a farmer gave him some sunflower seeds.

Jordi could not understand how life had once
seemed so sad and lonely to him, filled as it was with
so many beautiful things to discover. He kept bringing
more wildflowers to plant near the pond, and watered
them carefully every day. The moisture that surrounded
the pond made it easier to plant more seedlings, and
bit by bit the plants themselves began to spread.

Months and years went by. The apple branches had taken root and were now young trees that sprouted blossoms and bore fruit. Jordi gave apples to the farmer's children who brought him more seeds. The whole hillside began to bloom with greenery and flowers.